MW00887188

100 Ways To Wear A Scarf

2ND EDITION
Now with Step by Step Photos

Feel irresistible in your new look

Tonya L Butcher

Photography by Tonya Butcher
www. SilksbyTonya.com
Email: Info@SilksbyTonya.com

ISBN-13: 979-8703693889

What's new in this 2nd Edition:

1) I have added a new index by scarf size and added images with page numbers for easy indexing.

2) I have added step by step instructions with images to guide you every step of the way.

DEDICATION

I dedicate this book to my wonderful husband, Bill Butcher, who continues to be one of the most amazing and supportive men in the world. It has been incredible sharing my life and journey with you love.

ACKNOWLEDGMENTS

Thanks to my beautiful daughter, Amber Horn, and fellow artist and friend, Rose Hostetter, for adding your beauty to the scarves and allowing me to feature you.

Tonya Butcher

Record Your Favorites

Page # _____ Note _____

Page # _____ Note _____

Page # _____ Note _____

Page # _____ Note _____

Page # _____ Note _____

Page # _____ Note _____

Page # _____ Note _____

Page # _____ Note _____

Page # _____ Note _____

Page # _____ Note _____

Tonya Butcher

Introduction

Are you ready to learn many ways to wear your beautiful scarves? You will find just how wonderful scarves and wraps can be to increase your wardrobe and save you time and money.

In this book you will see many illustrations of my luxurious hand painted silk scarves. Even though I have used silk in my demonstrations, you can use any fabric of a similar size and weight to achieve the same look.

To see more of my hand painted silk scarf designs you may visit my website at www.SilksbyTonya.com

Please feel free to connect with me through my website to share photos of the looks you have been able to achieve with my techniques. I love making new connections.

Take care

enjoy your new look……

Tonya Butcher

Index

Tonya Butcher

Chapter 1 - 35" x 35" Scarves

Page 13

Page 14

Page 15

Page 16

Page 17

Page 18

Page 19

Page 20

Page 21

Page 22

Page 23

Page 24

Page 25

Page 26

Page 27

Page 28

Page 29

Page 30

Page 31

Page 32

Chapter 1 - 35" x 35" Scarves cont.

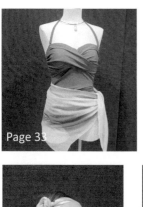
Page 33

Page 34

Page 35

Page 36

Page 37

Page 38

Page 39

Page 40

Page 41

Page 42

Page 43

Peacock Cowl Small w/ Scarf Pin

This design begins with a 35" x 35" square silk scarf. Fold the scarf into a triangle by joining the opposite corners together. Drape the point of the triangle in the front wrapping the 2 tails to the back. Cross the ends in the back and bring the points to the front. Allow the tails to hang over the point of the triangle. Attach the scarf pin on the tails to hold the design secure.

Beautiful!

See video #1 on my website
www.SilksbyTonya.com

35" x 35" hand painted silk scarf and hand hammered scarf pin

This is a great look under a blazer for the office.

Step by Step

1) Beginning with a square, fold into a triangle

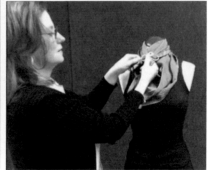

2) Place the point in the front, cross the tails in the back

3) Bring the tails to the front

4) Secure tails with clip or tie them

Peacock Shoulder Shawl Small

This design begins with a 35" x 35" square silk scarf. Fold the scarf into a triangle by joining the opposite corners together. Drape the long part of the triangle around the neck with the two points of the

triangle in the front. This is a lovely way to wear a scarf as a shawl.

See video #2 on my website
www.SilksbyTonya.com

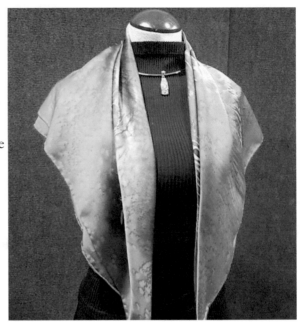

35" x 35" hand painted silk scarf

Step by Step

1) Beginning with a square scarf, fold into a triangle

2) Place the point of the triangle in the back

3) Drape the 2 long tails of the triangle over the shoulders to the front

Elegant Top Small

This design begins with a 35" x 35" square silk scarf. Fold the scarf into a triangle by joining the opposite corners together. Drape the long part of the triangle around the chest with the two points of the triangle to the back. Tie the two ends in a double knot in the back. Allow the point of the triangle to hang in the front.

You are sure to turn many heads in this design.

See video #3 on my website
www.SilksbyTonya.com

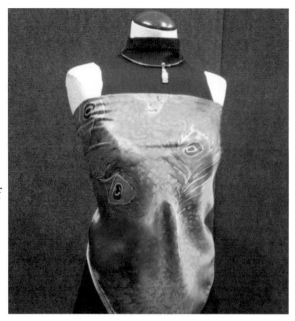

35" x 35" hand painted silk scarf

Step by Step

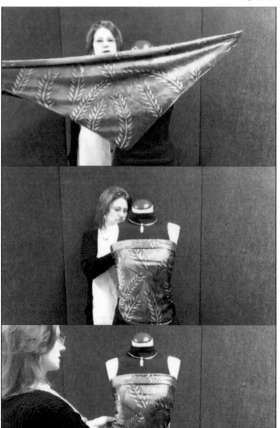

1) Beginning with a square scarf, fold into a triangle

2) Bring the 2 long ends of the triangle to the back and tie

3) Adjust

15

Side Neck Tie

This design begins with a 35" x 35" square silk scarf. Fold the scarf into a triangle by joining the opposite corners together. From the center of the triangle fold the scarf like a fan to form a narrow strip. Wrap the scarf from the center around the neck and place a single knot on the side allowing one tail to hang to the front and one to the back.

Great Job!

See video #4 on my website
www.SilksbyTonya.com

35" x 35" hand painted silk scarf

This is such a sophisticated look and soooo simple.

Step by Step

1) Start with a square scarf

2) Fold into a triangle

3) Starting at the long side of the triangle, fan or accordion fold into a narrow strip

4) Place center of narrow strip at side of neck

5) Holding the front tail straight out to the side, cross the back tail over the front

6) Bring the tail from the side down through the neck hole allowing it to hang to the back

Front Tie Top

This design begins with a 35" x 35" square silk scarf. Fold the scarf into a triangle by joining the opposite corners together. Drape the long part of the triangle around the back and bring the ends around the breast. Tie the two ends in a double knot in the front. Allow the point of the triangle to hang in the back.

Congrats on another beautiful design.

See video #5 on my website
www.SilksbyTonya.com

35" x 35" hand painted silk scarf

Step by Step

1) Begin with a square, fold into a triangle

2) Place point of triangle in the back

3) Bring the points of the triangle around to the front

4) Tie a knot securing on breasts

Cowl w/ Tails

This design begins with a 35" x 35" square silk scarf. Fold the scarf into a triangle by joining the opposite corners together. Drape the long part of the triangle around the neck from the front to the back. Cross the ends in the back and bring the points to the front. Allow the tails to hang over the point of the triangle. This design looks great under a jacket.

See video #6 on my website
www.SilksbyTonya.com

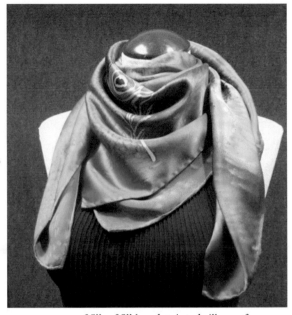

35" x 35" hand painted silk scarf

This look can also be achieved with a much larger scarf.

Step by Step

1) Beginning with a square scarf, fold into a triangle

2) Place the point of the triangle on the front of the chest

3) Cross the tails of the triangle in the back

4) Drape the tails in the front

Side Sash Tie

This design begins with a 35" x 35" square silk scarf. Fold the scarf into a triangle by joining the opposite corners together. Drape the long part of the triangle over one shoulder allowing the point of the triangle to drape down one arm. Tie the two ends in a double knot on the side just under the breast.

Simply irresistible!

See video #7 on my website
www.SilksbyTonya.com

I love the movement as it drapes over the arm.

35" x 35" hand painted silk scarf

Step by Step

1) Beginning with a square scarf, fold into a triangle

2) Place the triangle on the shoulder with the point running down the arm

3) Bring the long tails of the triangle to the opposite side of the point

4) Tie a double knot to secure

Side Waste Tie

This design begins with a 35" x 35" square silk scarf. Fold the scarf into a triangle by joining the opposite corners together. Drape the long part of the triangle around the waste with the two points of the triangle on the hip. Tie the two ends at the hip forming a waste wrap. This design looks great over a dress or bathing suite. Have fun sporting this look.

See video #8 on my website
www.SilksbyTonya.com

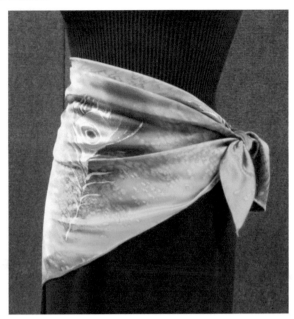

35" x 35" hand painted silk scarf

Step by Step

1) Beginning with a square scarf, fold into a triangle

2) Place point of triangle on side of hip

3) Tie a knot on opposite hip from point

4) Adjust

Shoulder Tie w/ Scarf Pin

This design begins with a 35" x 35" square silk scarf. Fold the scarf into a triangle by joining the opposite corners together. Drape the long part of the triangle over one shoulder allowing the point of the triangle to drape down over the shoulder and upper arm. Cross the points at the opposite shoulder allowing them to overlap. Attach your scarf pin over both tails allowing one to hang in the front and one in the back. Fantastic job!

See video #9 on my website
www.SilksbyTonya.com

35" x 35" hand painted silk scarf and hand hammered scarf pin

Step by Step

1) Begin with a square scarf

2) Fold into a triangle

3) Place point on shoulder

4) Drape front tail to the back

5) Drape back tail to the front

6) Gather both tails at neck & secure with a scarf pin

7) Pull both tails and pin slightly to the front

Shoulder Shawl Small w/ Scarf Pin

This design begins with a 35" x 35" square silk scarf. Fold the scarf into a triangle by joining the opposite corners together. Drape the long part of the triangle around the neck with the two points of the triangle in the front. Attach your scarf pin to both tails at the breast line. This is an elegant and easy way to wear a scarf. Enjoy….

See video #10 on my website
www.SilksbyTonya.com

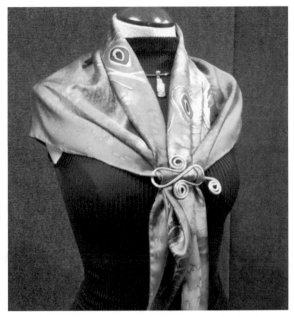

35" x 35" hand painted silk scarf
and hand hammered scarf pin

Step by Step

1) Begin with a square scarf, fold into a triangle

2) Place point of triangle in the back

3) Drape the long tails of the triangle over the shoulders and in the front.

4) Draw both tails together and secure with scarf pin

Neck Tie Medium

This design begins with a 35" x 35" long silk scarf. Fold the scarf into a triangle by joining the opposite corners together. Drape the point of the triangle at the back and the two points around to the front. Holding one tail in your hand take the other tail over the top of the other and around (twice). Then take it up through the neck and down through the second wrap you made. Pull it down to secure it.

Just like a neck tie.

See video #30 on my website
www.SilksbyTonya.com

35" x 35" hand painted silk scarf

Step by Step

1) Begin with a large square scarf, fold into a triangle

2) Drape over shoulders with point in the back

3) Cross left tail over right and wrap under

4) Bring tail over and under once more

5) Bring wrapped tail up through neck hole and down through loop made by wrapping

6) Pull to tighten

Southwest Elegance

This design begins with a 35" x 35" square silk scarf. Fold the scarf into a triangle by joining the opposite corners together. Place the point of the triangle in the front and cross the tails in the back and bring them around to the front. Tie a double knot on the side of the neck.

You go cowgirl!

See video #44 on my website
www.SilksbyTonya.com

35" x 35" hand painted silk scarf

Step by Step

1) Begin with a medium square scarf, fold into a triangle

2) Place the point of the triangle in the front and cross the tails in the back

3) Bring both tails to the front and gather them at the side of the neck

4) Tie a double knot in the tails at the side of the neck

Twisted Cowl

This design begins with a 35" x 35" square silk scarf. Fold the scarf into a triangle by joining the opposite corners together. By rolling the scarf from the point of the triangle fold into a narrow strip. Wrap the strip around the neck and tie at the side in a single knot. Twist the two tails around each other until you reach a few inches from the end and tie a single knot in the twisted strand. Wrap the twisted tails around the front of the neck and tuck one end around the strip around the neck and tie a single knot. Great job, you are done!

35" x 35" hand painted silk scarf

See video #46 on my website

Step by Step

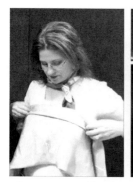   

1)   Begin with a square scarf, fold it into a triangle 2) Starting at point, roll scarf into a narrow strip
       3) Wrap strip around neck and tie a single knot on side

4) Twist tails until you are about 4 inches from the end

5) Tie a double knot securing the tails to the side of the strip around the neck

Summer Fun

This design begins with a 35" x 35 square silk scarf. Grab the point of one of the corners in your fingers and with the other hand gather the fabric into a bunch about 16 inches down the scarf from the point. Wrap the gathered fabric around the neck and tie the point in a double knot around the gathered fabric. Move the knot to the side of the neck and allow the rest of the scarf to hang to the front.

You are one of a kind. Great job!

See video #49 on my website
www.SilksbyTonya.com

35" x 35" hand painted silk scarf

Step by Step

1) Begin with a medium square scarf

2) Grabbing the scarf at one corner, slide your hang down gathering the scarf just long enough to go around the neck

3) Place the gathered portion of the scarf around the neck

4) Tie a double knot securing the short end to the long end

5) Spin the scarf so that the knot is at the side

26

Southwest Fun

This design begins with a 35" x 35" square silk scarf. Fold the scarf into a triangle by joining the opposite corners together. Roll the scarf from the point into a long narrow strip. Wrap the scarf around the neck, crossing the ends and wrap a second time. Bring the ends together at the side and tie a double knot.

Southwest Belle, just beautiful!

See video #50 on my website www.SilksbyTonya.com

35"x 35" hand painted silk scarf

Step by Step

1) Begin with a medium square scarf, fold into a triangle.

2) Starting at the point, roll the scarf into a narrow strip

3) Place the strip around the neck from the front, crossing in the back

4) Bringing the tails forward

5) Tie a double knot in tails at side

Head Wrap

This design begins with a 35" x 35"square silk scarf. Fold the scarf into a triangle by placing the opposite corners together. Wrap the scarf around your head at your forehead allowing the point to hang in the back. Tie the tails in a double knot at the back of your head.

Great summer look, sport it!

See video #53 on my website
www.SilksbyTonya.com

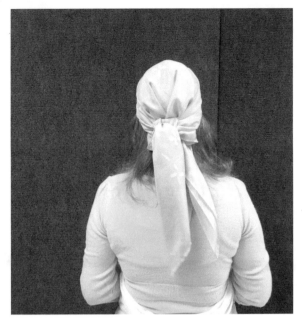

35" x 35" hand painted silk scarf

Step by Step

1) Begin with a medium square scarf, fold it into a triangle

2) Wrap the long part of the triangle at center around the head front to back

3) Bring the tails together in the back

4) Tie a double knot in the tails in the back

Side Tie Head Wrap

This design begins with a 35" x 35" square silk scarf. Fold the scarf into a triangle by joining the opposite corners together. Wrap the long part of the triangle around the front of the head and the point on the side that you want the tie. Take the tails to the side and tie a double knot. Allow the tails to hang to the side.

Grab your shades and rock this look!

See video #59 on my website
www.SilksbyTonya.com

35" x 35" hand painted silk scarf

Step by Step

1) Begin with a medium square scarf, fold into a triangle

2) Place the center of the long side of the triangle in the front of the forehead and bring the tails and point to the back

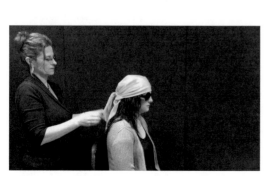

3) Tie a double knot in the tails and allow them to sit on top of the point

4) Spin the entire scarf around so that the knot is on the side that you prefer

Elegant Neck Design

This design begins with a 35" x 35" square silk scarf. Fold the scarf into a triangle by joining the opposite corners together. Roll from the point forming a narrow strip. Wrap the narrow strip around the neck at the center of the scarf. Tie a single knot on the side allowing both tails to hang in the front.

Simple elegance!

See video #61 on my website
www.SilksbyTonya.com

35" x 35" hand painted silk scarf

Step by Step

1) Begin with a medium square scarf and fold into a triangle

2) Form a narrow strip by rolling or folding

3) Place narrow strip around the neck

4) Tie a single knot at the side of the neck and allow the tails to hang in the front

Sarong Side Tie w/ Scarf Pin

This design begins with a 35" x 35" square silk scarf. Fold the scarf into a triangle by joining the opposite corners together. Take the long side of the triangle around the waste allowing the point to hang on the hip. Cross the two tails at the opposite hip and attach your scarf pin to secure.

Grab your beach bag, you look great!

See video #64 on my website
www.SilksbyTonya.com

35"x 35" hand painted silk scarf

and hand hammered scarf pin

Step by Step

1) Begin with a medium square scarf and fold into a triangle

2) Drape triangle around waistline with the point at the side

3) Bringing the tails to the opposite side as the point, cross the back tail over the front

4) Tie in a knot or secure with a scarf pin

Summer Top

This design begins with a 35" x 35" square silk scarf. Take the two top corners of the square and wrap around neck from front to back and tie a double knot in the back. Take the two bottom corners around the waist and tie in a double knot at the lower back.

Vuala, you have a summer cover up.

See video #68 on my website
www.SilksbyTonya.com

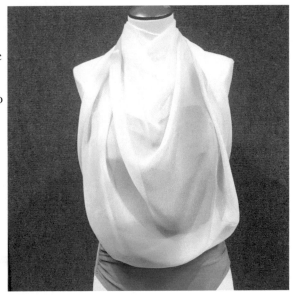

35"x 35" hand painted silk scarf

Step by Step

1) Begin with a medium square scarf and place the scarf on the front of the body

2) Grab the top 2 corners and tie them in a double knot at the back of the neck

3) Grab the bottom 2 corners and take them to the back

4) Tie a double knot in the bottom 2 corners at the back of waistline

Sarong Bathing Suit Cover Side Tie

This design begins with a 35" x 35" square silk scarf. Fold the scarf into a triangle by joining the opposite corners together. Wrap the scarf around the waist allowing the point to hang at one hip. Tie a knot on the opposite hip.

Enjoy your new bathing suit cover up, you look great!

See video #69 on my website
www.SilksbyTonya.com

35" x 35" hand painted silk scarf

Step by Step

1) Begin with a medium square scarf and fold into a triangle

2) Drape triangle around waistline with the point at the side pointing downward

3) Bringing the tails to the opposite side as the point, cross the back tail over the front

4) Tie in a knot or secure with a scarf pin

Knotted Noggin

This design begins with a 35" x 35" square silk scarf. Fold the scarf into a triangle by joining the opposite corners together. Roll the scarf from the point to form a long strip. Wrap the strip from the back of the neck to the top of the forehead. Tie a

double knot on the top of the head and tuck the tails behind the strip.

Beautiful and fun!

See video #82 on my website
www.SilksbyTonya.com

35"x 35" hand painted silk scarf

Step by Step

1) Begin with a square scarf, fold into a triangle

2) Roll the scarf from the point creating a narrow strip

3) Place the scarf at the base of the back of the neck

4) Bring both tails to the top of the head at the hair line

5) Tie a double knot in the tails at the hair line

6) Tuck both tails under the scarf on the sides

34

Chill'n Head Wrap

This design begins with a 35" x 35" square silk scarf. Fold the scarf into a triangle by joining the opposite corners together. Place the triangle around the front of the head with the point in the back. Tie the tails in the back over the point of the triangle.

Grab your shades....

See video #83 on my website
www.SilksbyTonya.com

35" x 35" hand painted silk scarf

Step by Step

1) Begin with a medium square scarf, fold into a triangle

2) Place the long end of the triangle at the forehead

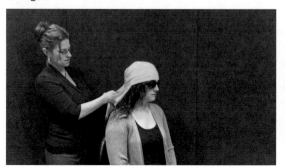

3) Tie a double knot in both tails at the back of the head

4) Allow both tails to hang in the back over the point

Twisted Noggin Wrap

This design begins with a 35" x 35" square silk scarf. Fold the scarf into a triangle by joining the two opposite corners. Starting at the point of the triangle, roll the scarf into a long strip. Wrap the strip around the head and tie in a single knot. Twist the tails until you reach the end of the tails. Wrap the twist around the head and tuck the ends.

You are amazing, great job….

See video #87 on my website
www.SilksbyTonya.com

35" x 35" hand painted silk scarf

Step by Step

1) Begin with a medium square scarf, fold into a triangle

2) From the point of the triangle, roll into a narrow strip

3) Wrap the scarf around the head

4) Tie a single knot on the right side of the head

5) Twist the tails until you reach the end of the tails

6) Wrap the twist around the front of the head and tuck under scarf on the left side

Flowering Head Wrap

This design begins with a 35" x 35" square silk scarf. Form a triangle by joining the two opposite corners. Starting at the point of the triangle, roll the scarf into a narrow strip. Wrap the strip around the head and tie a single knot on the side. Twist the ends until a bun begins to form. Tuck the ends of the scarf into the bun.

Cute look, great job!

See video #90 on my website
www.SilksbyTonya.com

35"x 35" hand painted silk scarf

Step by Step

1) Begin with a medium square scarf, fold into a triangle

2) From the point, roll into a narrow strip

3) Wrap scarf around the back of the head and bring point together at the top side of the head

4) Tie a single knot in the tails at the side top of the head

5) Twist the tails until they form a coil (flower)

6) Tuck the ends of the tails into the coil (flower)

Classic Head Wrap

This design begins with a 35" x 35" square silk scarf. Form a triangle by joining the two opposite corners together. Wrap the long part of the triangle around the face with the point of the triangle at the back. Tie a single knot in the tails under the chin.

Lovely classic look...

See video #93 on my website
www.SilksbyTonya.com

35" x 35" hand painted silk scarf

Step by Step

1) Begin with a medium square scarf, fold into a traingle

2) Drape scarf over the head with the point going down the back

3) Tie a single or double knot in the tails under the chin

Twisted Head Wrap

This design begins with a 35" x 35" square silk scarf. Form a triangle by joining the two opposite corners. Starting at the point of the triangle, roll the scarf into a narrow strip. Wrap the scarf around the head and tie a single knot at the back of the head. Twist each tail and bring them to the front joining the two by tying a double knot in the front.

Awesome job!

See video #94 on my website
www.SilksbyTonya.com

35"x 35" hand painted silk scarf

Step by Step

1) Begin with a medium square scarf, fold into a triangle

2) From the point, roll into a narrow strip

3) Wrap the strip around the head with the center at the forehead

4) Tie a single knot in the tails at the back of the head

5) Twist both tails separately

6) Bring the twisted tails to the front and tie a double knot at the forehead

Adorn A Handbag

This design begins with a 35" x 35" square silk scarf. Form a triangle by joining the two opposite corners. Starting at the point of the triangle, roll the scarf into a narrow strip. Wrap the scarf around the strap of any hand bag and vuala, you have added a pop of color to your outfit.

You've done it again, great job!

See video #96 on my website
www.SilksbyTonya.com

35"x 35" hand painted silk scarf

Step by Step

The possibilities are endless, get creative, spice up a simple bag by tying a beautiful scarf around it.

Fun Summer Top

This design begins with a 35" x 35" square silk scarf. Form a triangle by joining the two opposite corners. Place the long side of the triangle around the back of the head allowing the point to drape over the face. Bring the tails around to the front and tie in a single knot on the side of the head. Take the point over the knot and tuck it under the knot created on the top of the head. Using the tails, tie a bow on the top of the head.

Beautiful!

See video #97 on my website www.SilksbyTonya.com

35" x 35" hand painted silk scarf

Step by Step

1) Begin with a medium square scarf, fold into a triangle

2) Place the long side of the triangle around the back of the head allowing the point to drape over the face

3) Tie a single knot in the tails at the top of the head

4) Tuck the point around and under the knot just created

5) Tie a single knot in the tails on top of the head and create a bow

6) Fluff the bow

Classic Bow

This design begins with a 35" x 35" square silk scarf. Form a triangle by joining the two opposite corners. Starting at the point, roll the scarf into a long narrow strip. Wrap the scarf around the head joining the ends at the top or side of the head and tie a bow.

Wonderful Job!

See video #99 on my website www.SilksbyTonya.com

35" x 35" hand painted silk scarf

Step by Step

1) Begin with a medium square scarf, fold into a triangle

2) From the point, roll into a narrow strip

3) Wrap the strip around the back of the head at the base of the neck and bring tails together at the top of the head

4) Tie a bow at the top of the head, fluffing the bow

Kick'n Head Wrap

This design begins with a 35" x 35" square silk scarf. Form a triangle by joining the two opposite corners. Wrap the long part of the triangle around the head at the brow and join them in the back. Cross the two ends in the back and bring them around to the front. Tie a bow at the front or side of the head.

Very nice job!

See video #100 on my website
www.SilksbyTonya.com

35"x 35" hand painted silk scarf

Step by Step

2) Begin with a medium square scarf, fold into a triangle

2) Place long part of triangle at the forehead

3) Cross tails in the back

4) Bring both tails back around to the front

5) Tie a bow in the front of the head

Chapter 2 - 14" x 72" Scarves

Page 46

Page 47

Page 48

Page 49

Page 50

Page 51

Page 52

Page 53

Page 54

Page 55

Page 56

Page 57

Page 58

Page 59

Page 60

Page 61

Page 62

Page 63

Page 64

Page 65

Chapter 2 - 14" x 72" Scarves cont.

Page 66

Page 67

Page 68

Page 69

Page 70

Page 71

Page 72

Page 73

Page 74

Page 75

Page 76

Shoulder Sash Tie w/ Scarf Pin

This design begins with a 14" x 72" long silk scarf. Bring the scarf around the side and join the tails together at the opposite shoulder. Attach your scarf pin to both tails securing them at the shoulder. Allow the tails to drape over the shoulder and down the arm. Beautiful job!

See video #11 on my website
www.SilksbyTonya.com

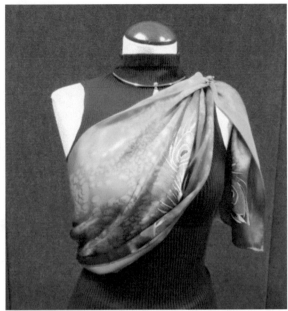

This is a beautiful way to show off a hand painted piece of silk without wearing it around your neck.

14" x 72" hand painted silk scarf and hand hammered scarf pin

Step by Step

1) Beginning with a long narrow scarf, wrap center of scarf at side waist

2) Bring ends of scarf up from waist to opposite shoulder

3) Gather ends at shoulder

4) Secure with a scarf pin and allow tails to drape over the arm

Bow Tie Top

This design begins with a 14" x 72" long silk scarf. Take the scarf around the body from the back to the front. Bring the scarf ends together in the front at the breast line. Tie the scarf in a bow paying attention to tie it tight enough that it wont come down.

Perfect!

See video #12 on my website
www.SilksbyTonya.com

14" x 72" hand painted silk scarf

This is such a cute way to create a top

Step by Step

1) Begin with a long narrow scarf,

2) place the center at the middle back with both ends in front

3) Gather over left breast then right

4) Tie in the center creating a bow

5) Pull the loops of the bow so they are both large

6) fluff the bow

Neck Tie Long

This design begins with a 14" x 72" long silk scarf. Drape the scarf around the neck allowing one end to be longer than the other. While holding the shorter end, take the longer end and cross it over the shorter one (twice). Bring the long end up through the V created at the neck and down through the second wrap you have created around the shorter end. Tighten the design by pulling the long tail down. Just like a neck tie.

Sure to stay in place…

See video #17 on my website
www.SilksbyTonya.com

14" x 72" hand painted silk scarf

Step by Step

1) Center long scarf on neck

2) Cross left over right

3) Bring crossed tail under

4) Cross left over right again

5) Bring wrapped tail up through neck hole

6) Pull wrapped tail down through loop made by wrapping

7) Pull tight and adjust

48

Shoulder Sash Wrap Top

This design begins with a 14" x 72" long silk scarf. Hold the point of one end at the center of the back. Bring the scarf around the side at an angle from your lower back around the breast and over the shoulder. Then bringing it around the waist a second time ending at the middle back where you started with the other end. Tie a double knot in the points that meet in the back. Awesome job!

See video #24 on my website
www.SilksbyTonya.com

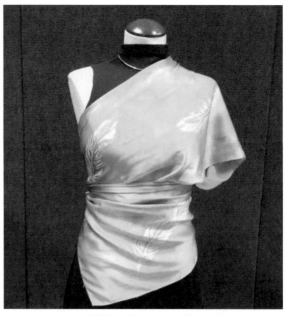

14" x 72" hand painted silk scarf

Step by Step

1) Begin with a long narrow scarf, Place the end of the scarf at the back of the hip and wrap around the shoulder.

2) Wrap diagonal across the body and then around the waist

3) Wrap the scarf around the hip and belly

4) Tie a double knot in the top ends of the scarf at the back hip

Infinity Scarf

This design begins with a 14" x 72" long silk scarf. Take the opposite corners together and tie them in a double knot as close to the end as you can. Drape the long circle around your neck. Twist the design once and drape the created loop around your neck a second time.

Congrats, you just created an infinity scarf.

See video #28 on my website
www.SilksbyTonya.com

14" x 72" hand painted silk scarf

Step by Step

1) Begin with a long narrow scarf

2) Grab the two opposite corners

3) Tie a knot in the two ends, this creates a circle

4) Drape the circle around the neck

5) Twist the front portion of the circle creating an X

6) Wrap the second circle created around the neck and adjust

Loopy

This design begins with a 14" x 72" long silk scarf. Fold the scarf in half. Drape the folded scarf around your neck. Pull the end of the scarf through the loop that was created at the fold. Adjust the scarf.

Rock that silk....

See video #31 on my website
www.SilksbyTonya.com

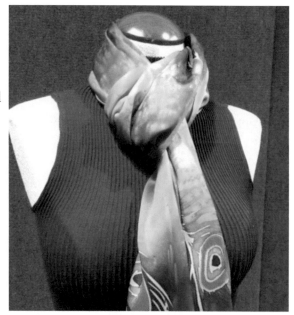

14" x 72" hand painted silk scarf

Step by Step

1) Begin with a long narrow scarf, find the center, fold the scarf creating a loop

2) Holding onto the center of the scarf, wrap the looped scarf around the neck placing your hand through the loop grabbing tails

3) Pull both tails through the loop

4) pull tails to tighten

Single Wrap

This design begins with a 14" x 72" long silk scarf. Drape the scarf around your neck. Wrap it once around your neck allowing both tails to hang in the front. Adjust to the length you want each tail.

Looking good!

See video #32 on my website
www.SilksbyTonya.com

14" x 72" hand painted silk scarf

Step by Step

1) Beginning with a long narrow scarf, drape the scarf around the neck

2) Wrap the scarf all the way around the neck one time

3) Allow both tails to hang in the front

Single Neck Wrap w/ Scarf Pin

This design begins with a 14" x 72" long silk scarf. Drape the scarf around your neck. Wrap it once around your neck allowing both tails to hang in the front. Adjust to the length you want each tail. Attach your scarf pin where the two tails come together.

Awesome job!

See video #33 on my website
www.SilksbyTonya.com

14" x 72" hand painted silk scarf

and hand hammered scarf pin

Step by Step

1) Begin with a long narrow scarf, wrap it around the neck one time

2) Allowing both tails to hang in the front

3) Gather both tails in front and secure with scarf pin or tie them

Loop and Purl

This design begins with a 14" x 72" long silk scarf. Fold the scarf in half, with one end longer than the other. Hold your hand inside the loop created by the fold. Drape the scarf around your neck. Place your hand through the loop picking up the longer tail. Pulling it half way through the loop creating another loop. Place your hand inside the new loop and pick up the shorter tail, pulling it all the way through. Adjust the tightness.

Well done!

See video #34 on my website www.SilksbyTonya.com

14" x 72" hand painted silk scarf

Step by Step

1) Begin with a long scarf, fold it in half, leaving one side slightly longer

2) Hold your hand inside the loop created by folding the scarf

3) pick up the longer tail and pull it slightly through the loop (this creates another loop)

4) Place your hand through the loop just created and grab the shorter tail

5) Pull the shorter tail through the loop

6) Adjust

Front Tie Top

This design begins with a 14" x 72" long silk scarf. Drape the scarf around your back bringing the ends together at the front. Tie a double knot tightly at the breast line and allow the tails to hang in the front.

Way to go, Rock this look!

See video #35 on my website
www.SilksbyTonya.com

14" x 72" hand painted silk scarf

Step by Step

1) Begin with a long narrow scarf

2) Find the center and place it around the back

3) Gather both tails at the center of the breast line

4) Tie a double knot to secure

Front Drape Design

This design begins with a 14" x 72" long silk scarf. Drape the scarf around your neck. Adjust the length of each tail to your liking.

You look fantastic!

See video #36 on my website www.SilksbyTonya.com

14" x 72" hand painted silk scarf

Step by Step

1) Begin with a long narrow scarf

2) Drape scarf around neck placing tails in front

3) Adjust to your liking

If you like these silk scarves, many of them can be ordered from my website www.SilksbyTonya.com

Shoulder Wrap w/ Scarf Pin

This design begins with a 14" x 72" long silk scarf. Drape the scarf around your shoulders, bringing the ends together at the front. Attach your scarf pin just under the breast line. Allow the tails to hang in the front.

Very elegant, nice job!

See video #37 on my website
www.SilksbyTonya.com

14" x 72" hand painted silk scarf

and hand hammered scarf pin

Step by Step

1) Begin with a long narrow scarf, find the center and drape it over the back of the shoulders

2) Placing the scarf low on the shoulders is key to this look

3) Bringing tails around to the front, Gather them just below the breast line

4) Secure tails with a scarf pin or tie them

Loop and Tuck Wrap

This design begins with a 14" x 72" long silk scarf. Fold the scarf in half. Wrap the scarf around your neck, holding your hand in the loop created by the fold. Place your hand through the loop and pick up one of the tails drawing it all the way through the loop. Place your hand up through the bottom bar of the loop created by the fold and draw through the other tail.

You rock!

See video #38 on my website
www.SilksbyTonya.com

14" x 72" hand painted silk scarf

Step by Step

1) Begin with a long narrow scarf, fold it in half placing your hand inside the fold

2) Draw one of the tails UP through the loop made by the fold

3) Draw the other tail DOWN through the same loop

Back Draping Wrap

This design begins with a 14" x 72" long silk scarf. Drape the scarf around your shoulders, allowing the tails to drape to the back.

Beautiful!

See video #39 on my website
www.SilksbyTonya.com

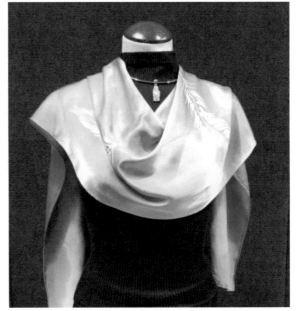

14" x 72" hand painted silk scarf

Step by Step

1) Begin with a long narrow scarf

2) Find the center of the scarf and drape it in the front of the body

3) Allow the tails to drape down the back

Depending on the type of fabric you may need to secure it with a pin. Silk tends to be rather slippery, but this style works well with fabrics that have a little more grab .

Front Draping Single Wrap

This design begins with a 14" x 72" long silk scarf. Take the center of the scarf holding it at the front of the neck. Taking the tails to the back and cross them. Bring the tails back to the front. Allow them to drape in the front.

Nice new look!

See video #40 on my website
www.SilksbyTonya.com

14" x 72" hand painted silk scarf

Step by Step

1) Begin with a long narrow scarf

2) Place the scarf around the neck bringing the end to about the waist line

3) Wrap the scarf around the neck one time allowing it to hang lower down the neckline

4) The wrapped end should be shorter than the other.

Twisted Loop

This design begins with a 14" x 72" long silk scarf. Fold the scarf in half. Place the folded scarf around your neck, holding your hand in the loop created by the fold. Draw both tails through the loop. Twist the loop to create a second loop and draw the tails through the second loop.

Lovely job!

See video #41 on my website
www.SilksbyTonya.com

14" x 72" hand painted silk scarf

Step by Step

1) Begin with a long narrow scarf, find the center

2) Fold the scarf in half and place hand in fold

3) Pull both tails through loop created by the fold

4) Grabbing the loop twist it once creating a second loop

5) Draw both tails through the second loop

Front Crossing Top

This design begins with a 14" x 72" long silk scarf. Drape the scarf around your neck and cross the tails over each breast making an X. Bring both tails to the back and tie in a double knot to secure.

Nice pop of color….

See video #42 on my website
www.SilksbyTonya.com

14" x 72" hand painted silk scarf

Step by Step

1) Begin with a long narrow scarf, find the center and place it around the neck

2) Cross the tails in the front of the neckline

3) Open up the scarf so that each tail covers one breast and wrap each tail around to the back

4) Tie a double knot in the back

Braided Design

This design begins with a 14" x 72" long silk scarf. Place the center of the scarf at the front of the neck. Take both tails to the back. Cross the tails in the back and bring them to the front. Create a loop in the front by taking the center piece at the neck, pull it forward and twist it once. Now take one of the tails up through the loop and the other down through the same loop.

You did it…. Great job!

See video #45 on my website
www.SilksbyTonya.com

14" x 72" hand painted silk scarf

Step by Step

1) Begin with a long narrow scarf, find the center of the scarf and place it over the neck

2) With the tails in the back, cross the loop in the front creating an X

3) cross the tails in the back and bring them forward

4) Take the left tail UP through the loop created

5) Pull the right tail DOWN through the same loop

5) Pull tails to adjust

Shoulder Cover Wrap Top

This design begins with a 14" x 72" long silk scarf. Wrap the scarf around your body above the breast line and cross the tails in the back and bring them over your shoulders. Bring the tails together at the neck and tie a double knot at the point of each tail.

Great summer look...

See video #48 on my website
www.SilksbyTonya.com

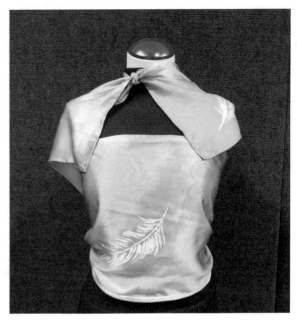

14" x 72" hand painted silk scarf

Step by Step

1) begin with a long narrow scarf

2) Place the center of the scarf in the front and wrap the tails to the back crossing them

3) Bring the tails up and over the shoulders

4) Tie a double knot in the corners of the tails at the neckline

Waste Wrap

This design begins with a 14" x 72" long silk scarf. Wrap the scarf around your waist from the front, crossing it in the back. Bring the ends to the front and tie in a double knot.

Awesome job!

See video #52 on my website
www.SilksbyTonya.com

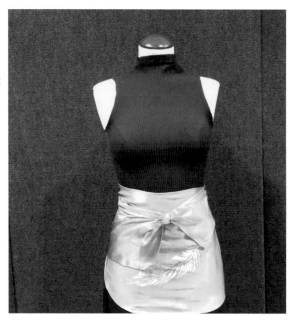

14"x 72" hand painted silk scarf

Step by Step

1) Begin with a long narrow scarf, find the center

2) Drape it around the front crossing the tails in the back

3) Bring the tails to the front

4) Grab the 2 points at the top and tie a double knot

Twisted X Top

This design begins with a 14" x 72" long silk scarf. Wrap the long scarf around the back. Bring the ends together and cross them at the breast line. Bring the ends around the neck and tie a double knot around the neck.

Awesome summer look....

See video #56 on my website
www.SilksbyTonya.com

14"x 72" hand painted silk scarf

Step by Step

1) Begin with a long narrow scarf, wrap in around the body (center at back)

2) Bring the tails to the front and gather them in the center at breast line

3) Twist the tails one time at the breast line

4) Bring the tails up and around the neck

5) Tie a double knot behind the neck to secure

Waist Wrap w/ Scarf Pin

This design begins with a 14" x 72" long silk scarf. Wrap the scarf around the waste at the center from back to front. Bring the tails together in the front and attach your scarf pin in the center, allowing the scarf to drape low in the front.

This creates an hour glass waste…. Enjoy!

See video #57 on my website
www.SilksbyTonya.com

14" x 72" hand painted silk scarf

and hand hammered scarf pin

Step by Step

1) Begin with a long narrow scarf, wrap it around the hips with the center at the back

2) Bring the tails forward and gather them in the front

3) overlap the left tail over the right tail in the front

4) Secure tails with a scarf pin

Front Sash w/ Scarf Pin

This design begins with a 14" x 72" long silk scarf. Drape the scarf over one shoulder and bring the tails together in the front on the opposite hip. Attach your scarf pin in the front of the hip.

Fun look, sport it!

See video #58 on my website
www.SilksbyTonya.com

14"x 72" hand painted silk scarf

and hand hammered scarf pin

Step by Step

1) Begin with a long narrow scarf

2) Place the center of the scarf on the right shoulder

3) Gather the tails together at the left hip

4) Overlap the back tail over the front tail

5) Secure tails at hip with a scarf pin or a double knot

Elegant Neck Wrap w/ Scarf Pin

This design begins with a 14" x 72" long silk scarf. Drape the scarf around the neck. Wrap it around your neck twice allowing the wrapped tail to hang to the back. Attach your scarf pin to the two tails at the neck to secure them.

Beautiful!

See video #60 on my website
www.SilksbyTonya.com

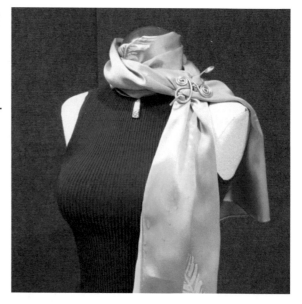

14"x 72" hand painted silk scarf

and hand hammered scarf pin

Step by Step

1) Begin with a long narrow scarf, place the center on one shoulder

2) Bring the tail from the back around the neck 2 times

3) Bring the wrapped tail all the way to the back

4) Secure both tails with a scarf pin allowing the wrapped tail to hang down the back

Bow Side Tie

This design begins with a 14" x 72" long silk scarf. Place the center of the scarf around the neck and tie a bow on the side of the neck allowing the tails to hang in the front.

Jazz up any outfit!

See video #65 on my website
www.SilksbyTonya.com

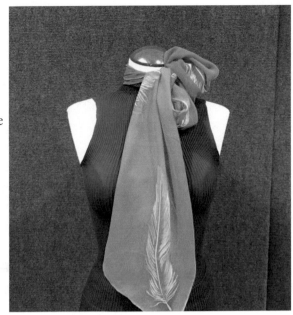

14" x 72" hand painted silk scarf

Step by Step

1) Begin with a long narrow scarf and drape it around the neck

2) Create a loop on both tails at the neckline

3) Tie a single knot in the loops

4) Puff out the loops

Double The Fun

This design begins with a 14" x 72" long silk scarf. Wrap the scarf around the neck front to back, crossing the tails in the back. Bring both tails to the front again and tie a single knot on the side of the neck allowing both tails to hang in the front.

Fantastic job, you look amazing!

See video #75 on my website
www.SilksbyTonya.com

14" x 72" hand painted silk scarf

Step by Step

1) Begin with a long narrow scarf and find the center

2) Wrap the scarf around the neck at the side

3) Wrap one tail back around so that both tails are in the front

4) Tie a single knot in both tails at the side of the neck

Shoulder Shrug w/ Scarf Pin

This design begins with a 14" x 72" long silk scarf. Wrap the scarf around the back and bring one tail around the neck and tie the two tails together in a single knot. Allow both tails to drape to the front and secure the tails with a scarf pin.

Beautiful!

See video #84 on my website
www.SilksbyTonya.com

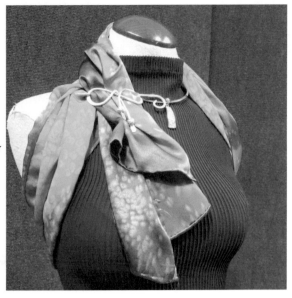

14"x 72" hand painted silk scarf

and hand hammered scarf pin

Step by Step

1) Begin with a long narrow scarf

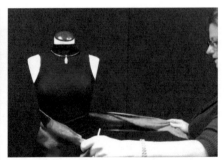

2) Place the scarf around the back

3) Pull the tails up in the front

4) Bring the left tail around the back of the neck and drape over right shoulder

5) Bring the right tail up to meet the other at the right shoulder

6) Either tie a double knot or secure with a scarf pin at right shoulder

Knotted V

This design begins with a 14" x 72" long silk scarf. Drape the scarf around the neck and allow the tails to hang in the front. Place a knot in the tails to secure.

Easy Elegance....

See video #85 on my website
www.SilksbyTonya.com

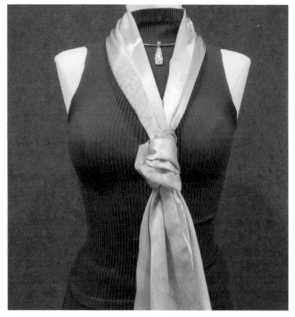

14" x 72" hand painted silk scarf

Step by Step

1) Begin with a long narrow scarf

2) Place the scarf around the neck

3) tie a single knot in both tails just below the neck line

4) Pull down on both tails to tighten to your desired look

Fashionable Head Wrap

This design begins with a 14" x 72" long silk scarf. Wrap the scarf around the head starting at the base of the neck in the back. Cross the ends in the front and bring the ends to the back and tie in a double knot. Allow the tails to hang to the back.

Easy and fun...

See video #91 on my website www.SilksbyTonya.com

14" x 72" hand painted silk scarf

Step by Step

1) Begin with a long narrow scarf

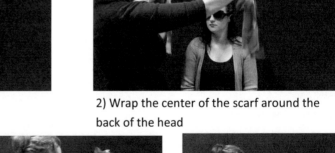

2) Wrap the center of the scarf around the back of the head

3) Cross the tails at the top of the head

4) Take both tails to the back of the head and tie in a double knot

5) Either allow tails to hang in the back or tuck them into sides of scarf

Fun Summer Top

This design begins with a 14" x 72" long silk scarf. Drape the scarf center around the neck and shoulders from the front to the back. Cross the tails in the back and bring the tails back to the front joining them at the breast line. Tie a double knot at the breast line.

Fun new look… Rock it!

See video #95 on my website
www.SilksbyTonya.com

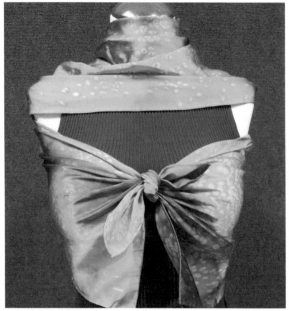

14" x 72" hand painted silk scarf

Step by Step

1) Begin with a long narrow scarf

2) Drape the center of the scarf around the front of the neck allowing the tails to hang in the back

3) Cross the tails in the back and bring them around to the front around the breast line

4) Tie a double knot in the tails at the breast line

#98 - Top Down

This design begins with a 14" x 72" long silk scarf. Wrap the scarf around the head, crossing at the front of the neck. Bring one of the tails around the neck joining it with the other tail. Tie a single knot at the side of the neck. Allow one tail to hang to the front and one to the back.

Looking good!

See video #98 on my website
www.SilksbyTonya.com

14"x 72" hand painted silk scarf

Step by Step

1) Begin with a long narrow scarf

2) Place scarf on top of the head

3) Cross the tails under the chin

4) Bring the left tail around the neck to the right shoulder

5) Tie a single knot in the tails at the right side of neck

Tonya Butcher

Chapter 3 - 44" x 44" Scarves

Page 80

Page 81

Page 82

Page 83

Page 84

Page 85

Page 86

Page 87

Page 88

Page 89

Page 90

Page 91

Page 92

Page 93

Page 94

Page 95

Page 96

Shoulder Shawl w/ Scarf Pin

This design begins with a 44" x 44" square silk scarf. Fold the scarf into a triangle by joining the opposite corners together. Drape the long part of the triangle over one shoulder allowing the point of the triangle to drape down over the shoulder and upper arm. Cross the points at the opposite shoulder allowing them to overlap. Attach your scarf pin over both tails allowing one to hang in the front and one in the back. Looking Good! One of my favorites.

See video #13 on my website
www.SilksbyTonya.com

44" x 44" hand painted silk scarf and hand hammered scarf pin

Step by Step

1) Begin with a large square scarf, fold into a triangle

2) Place the point on one shoulder, wrapping the tail from the back around to front

3) Cross the front tail over the same shoulder from front to back

4) Gather both tails at shoulder

5) Secure at shoulder with a scarf pin

6) Allow tails to drape in front and back exposing shoulder

Cowl Neck Large

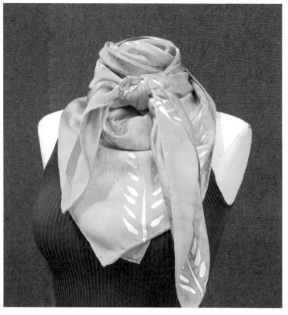

This design begins with a 44" x 44" square silk scarf. Fold the scarf into a triangle by joining the opposite corners together. Drape the long part of the triangle around the neck from the front to the back. With the point on the chest. Cross the ends in the back and bring the points to the front. Allow the tails to hang over the point of the triangle. Tie the tails in a double knot at the front of the neck.

Great look under a jacket.

See video #14 on my website
www.SilksbyTonya.com

44" x 44" hand painted silk scarf

Step by Step

1) Begin with a large square scarf   2) fold into a triangle   3) Drape the point of the triangle in the front

4) Cross the tails in the back   5) bring the tails to the front   6) Tie tails in a double knot to secure.

Sarong Side Tie

This design begins with a 44" x 44" square silk scarf. Fold the scarf into a triangle by joining the opposite corners together. Drape the long part of the triangle around the waste bringing the two points to the front. Tie the two ends at the hip allowing the knot to drape and hang down. Wear this over your favorite bathing suites for an elegant look.

See video #15 on my website
www.SilksbyTonya.com

44" x 44" hand painted silk scarf

This is a beautiful sarong for a cruise or elegant event.

Step by Step

1)   Begin with a square, fold into a triangle

2) Center the triangle on the hip

3) Gather the long tails on opposite hip from point

4) Tie a double knot on side using long tails

Shoulder Side Sash w/ Scarf Pin

This design begins with a 44" x 44" square silk scarf. Fold the scarf into a triangle by joining the opposite corners together. Drape the long part of the triangle over one shoulder allowing the point of the triangle to drape down one arm. Cross the ends at the hip and attach your scarf pin over both tails.

You've done it again… great job!

See video #16 on my website
www.SilksbyTonya.com

44" x 44" hand painted silk scarf

and hand hammered scarf pin

Step by Step

1) Begin with a square scarf and fold into a triangle

2) Drape the point of the triangle over the shoulder

3) Cross the back tail over the front tail

4) Secure with a scarf pin or tie a knot

Shoulder Shawl Large

This design begins with a 44" x 44" square silk scarf. Fold the scarf into a triangle by joining the opposite corners together. Drape the long part of the triangle around the neck with the two points of the triangle in the front.

Beautiful, you will love this look.

See video #18 on my website
www.SilksbyTonya.com

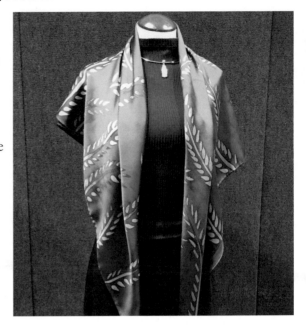

44" x 44" hand painted silk scarf

Step by Step

1) Begin with a large square scarf

2) Fold into a triangle

3) Wrap center of point around back of shoulders

4) Bring tails to the front

5) Fold neckline over to create a lapel

Cowl Neck Large w/ Tails

This design begins with a 44" x 44" square silk scarf. Fold the scarf into a triangle by joining the opposite corners together. Drape the long part of the triangle around the neck with the point on the chest. Cross the ends in the back and bring the points to the front. Allow the tails to hang over the point of the triangle.

Way to take your outfit from casual to WOW!

See video #19 on my website
www.SilksbyTonya.com

44" x 44" hand painted silk scarf

Step by Step

1) Begin with a large square scarf and fold into a triangle

2) Drape point of triangle in the front of chest

3) Cross tails in the back

4) Bring tails to the front and allow them to drape beside the point

Shoulder Shawl Large w/ Scarf Pin

This design begins with a 44" x 44" square silk scarf. Fold the scarf into a triangle by joining the opposite corners together. Drape the long part of the triangle around the neck with the two points of the triangle in the front. Attach your scarf pin to both tails at the breast line.

This is an elegant and easy way to wear a scarf. Enjoy….

See video #20 on my website
www.SilksbyTonya.com

44" x 44" hand painted silk scarf

and hand hammered scarf pin

Step by Step

1) Begin with a square scarf and fold into a triangle

2) Drape point of triangle in the back of shoulders

3) Fold down the neckline to create a lapel

4) Gather tails in front and secure with scarf pin or tie a knot

Cowl Neck Wrap Large w/ Scarf Pin

This design begins with a 44" x 44" square silk scarf. Fold the scarf into a triangle by joining the opposite corners together. Drape the long part of the triangle around the neck with the point on the chest. Cross the ends in the back and bring the points to the front. Allow the tails to hang over the point of the triangle. Attach the scarf pin on the tails to hold the design secure.

Awesome job!

See video #21 on my website
www.SilksbyTonya.com

44" x 44" hand painted silk scarf

This is a beautiful look under a blazer for the office.

Step by Step

1) Begin with a large square scarf, fold into a triangle

2) Drape the point of the triangle in front and over the chest

3) Cross the tails in the back

4) Bring the tails to the front

5) Secure tails with a scarf pin allowing it to lay on top of the point

Stole Wrap Large

This design begins with a 44" x 44" square silk scarf. Fold the scarf into a triangle by joining the opposite corners together. At the folded edge of the triangle, tie the ends together in a double knot. Step into the large circle you have created with the knot at your lower back. With the point of the triangle in front of you, take the point of the triangle over your head and allow the point to drape down your back.

Vuala, you have a jacket or shrug....

See video #22 on my website
www.SilksbyTonya.com

44" x 44" hand painted silk scarf

Step by Step

1) Begin with a large square scarf, fold it into a triangle

2) Tie a double knot in the ends of the tails forming an infinity style circular scarf

3) Place the circle around the waist with the knot at the middle back

4) Bring the point up and over the head so that the point is now in the back

5) Adjust

Here is a view from the back. You can see that the knot that was created is covered by the point.

In this view you can see how the arms hold it into place. Very stylish stole.

Elegant Top Large

This design begins with a 44" x 44" square silk scarf. Fold the scarf into a triangle by joining the opposite corners together. Drape the long part of the triangle around the breast with the two ends of the triangle to the back. Tie the two ends in a double knot in the back. Allow the point of the triangle to hang in the front.

Now go turn some heads!

See video #23 on my website
www.SilksbyTonya.com

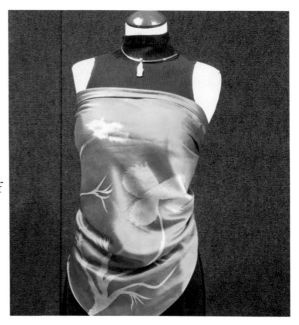

44" x 44" hand painted silk scarf

Step by Step

1) Begin with a large square scarf, fold it into a triangle

2) Place the long part of the triangle around the chest with the point down

3) Tie a double knot in the back to secure it in place

Jacket Wrap Large

This design begins with a 44" x 44" square silk scarf. Tie the top and bottom of the square together in a double knot. Repeat on both sides, this creates your arm holes. Drape the square over your shoulders and place your arms in the arm holes.

Beautiful!

See video #25 on my website
www.SilksbyTonya.com

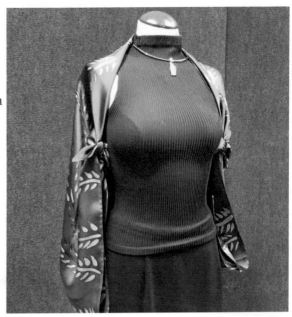

44" x 44" hand painted silk scarf

Step by Step

1) Begin with a large square scarf, place the scarf over the back of the shoulders

2) tie a double knot in the two ends on the left side of the body

3) tie a double knot in the two ends on the right side of the body

Here is a view of the arm hole that is created by tying the double knot on each side.

Front Cross Top w/ Scarf Pin

This design begins with a 44" x 44" square silk scarf. Fold the scarf into a triangle by joining the opposite corners together. Drape the long part of the triangle around the back and bring the ends around the breast. Attach your scarf pin at the center of the breast to secure the tails in place. Allow the point of the triangle to hang in the back.

Congrats on another beautiful design.

See video #26 on my website
www.SilksbyTonya.com

44" x 44" hand painted silk scarf

and hand hammered scarf pin

Step by Step

1) Begin with a square scarf, fold it into a triangle

2) Wrap around the back with the point down, bring the tails to the front

3) Cross the tails in the front

4) Gather both tails at center of breast line

5) Secure with a scarf pin at center of breast

Bathing Suit Wrap Large

This design begins with a 44" x 44" square silk scarf. Drape the square around your body and tie the top of the square together in a double knot above the breast.

Vuala, another great bathing suit cover.

See video #27 on my website
www.SilksbyTonya.com

44" x 44" hand painted silk scarf

Step by Step

1) Begin with a large square scarf

2) Place behind the body and bring around to the front

3) Grabbing corners at the top of the square, tie a double knot in the ends above breast line

Make sure to tie it tight enough so it doesn't slip down

Neck Tie Large

This design begins with a 44" x 44" square silk scarf. Fold the scarf into a triangle by joining the opposite corners together. Drape the point of the triangle at the back and the two points around to the front. Holding one tail in your hand take the other tail over the top of the other and around (twice). Then take it up through the neck and down through the second wrap you made. Pull it down to secure it.

Just like a neck tie.

See video #29 on my website
www.SilksbyTonya.com

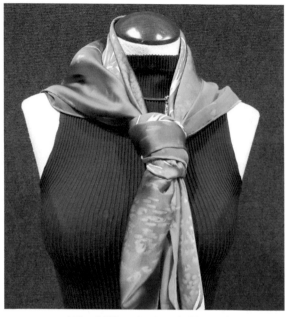

44" x 44" hand painted silk scarf

Step by Step

1) Begin with a large square scarf, fold into a triangle

2) Drape over shoulders with point in the back

3) Cross left tail over right

4) Bring tail under and wrap it over and under once more

5) Bring wrapped tail up through neck hole and down through loop made by wrapping

6) Pull to tighten

Sarong Front Tie

This design begins with a 44" x 44" square silk scarf. Fold the scarf into a triangle by joining the opposite corners together. Place the triangle around the waist with the point in the back. Tie the tails in the front in a double knot. Allow the knot to hang or drape in the front.

You are cruise ready…. Bon Voyage!

See video #81 on my website
www.SilksbyTonya.com

44" x 44" hand painted silk scarf

Step by Step

1) Begin with a large square scarf, fold into a triangle

2) Wrap the triangle around the waist line

3) Tie a double knot in the tails

4) wear it on the side or place the knot in the front

Turning Heads Top

This design begins with a 44" x 44" square silk scarf. Bring the two top corners together and tie behind the neck. Bring the two bottom corners together and tie around the waist. The back is exposed in this

design.

Fancy!

See video #88 on my website
www.SilksbyTonya.com

44"x 44" hand painted silk scarf

Step by Step

1) Begin with a large square scarf

2) Place the scarf in the front, Tie a double knot in the top 2 corners around the back of the neck

3) Tie a double knot in the bottom 2 corners around the waist

95

Bun Wrap Head Tie

This design begins with a 44" x 44" square silk scarf. Fold the scarf into a triangle by joining the two opposite corners. Wrap the long part of the triangle around the front of the head. Bring the tails around to the back and under the hair. Allowing the point of the triangle to hang on top of the hair. Including the hair with the tails and the point, twist all ends into a bun. Tuck the end of the tails into the bun. With shorter hair, this design can be done with a smaller scarf. Vuala, you're done....

See video #89 on my website
www.SilksbyTonya.com

44" x 44" hand painted silk scarf

Step by Step

1) Begin with a large square scarf, fold into a triangle

2) Place the long end of the triangle on the forehead, bring tails to the back

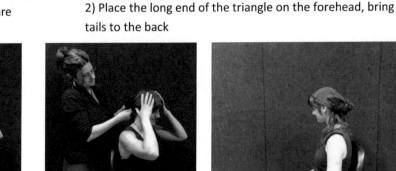

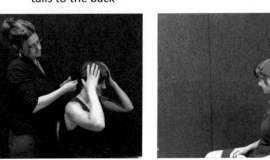

3) Tie a single knot in the tails, making sure the knot is under the point of the scarf.

4) Grabbing both tails and the point, twist scarf into a bun

5) Tuck the end of the tails into the bun

Chapter 4 - 22" x 22" Scarves

Page 100

Page 101

Page 102

Page 103

Page 104

Page 105

Trick Knot Front Tie

This design begins with a 22" x 22" square silk scarf. Fold the scarf into a triangle. Place the scarf around your neck with the point of the triangle in the back. Tie a knot about half way up one of the tails in the front. Before tightening the knot pull the other tail through the knot. Tighten the knot.

Awesome sauce!

See video #43 on my website
www.SilksbyTonya.com

22" x 22" hand painted silk scarf

Step by Step

Begin with a small square scarf, fold into a triangle

2) Drape the scarf around the neck with the point in the back and tie a knot in one of the tails

3) Using the loop created by tying the knot

4) Pull the other tail through the loop

5) Tighten the knot securing both ends together

6) Slide up to adjust

Bandanna Front Tie

This design begins with a 22" x 22" square silk scarf. Fold the scarf into a triangle and place the scarf around your neck with the point in the back. Bringing the tails together in the front, tie them into a double knot

You've done it again, great job!

See video #47 on my website
www.SilksbyTonya.com

22" x 22" hand painted silk scarf

Step by Step

1) Begin with a small square scarf, fold into a traiangle

2) Wrap triangle around the neck with point in the back and tails in the front

3) Gather the ends of the tails in the front

4) Tie a double knot in the tails at the neckline

Southwest Fun w/ Scarf Pin

This design begins with a 22" x 22 square silk scarf. Fold the scarf into a triangle by placing the opposite corners together. Wrap the scarf around your neck with the point of the triangle in the back. With the two tails draping to the front, attach the scarf pin to the tails at the neck. Done. Great job!

See video #51 on my website
www.SilksbyTonya.com

22" x 22" hand painted silk scarf

and hand hammered scarf pin

Step by Step

1) Begin with a small square scarf

2) Fold it into a triangle

3) Drape the triangle around the neck with the point in the back

4) Gather the points in the front and secure with scarf pin

Bandanna Back Tie

This design begins with a 22" x 22" square silk scarf. Fold the scarf into a triangle by joining the opposite corners. Wrap the triangle around your neck with the point in the front. Tie a double knot at the back of the neck. This look can be sported under a jacket for a professional look or to finish off a cowgirl look.

Grab your cowboy boots and hat.

See video #54 on my website
www.SilksbyTonya.com

22"x 22" hand painted silk scarf

Step by Step

1) Begin with a small square scarf, fold into a triangle

2) Place the point of the triangle on the front of the neck and tie a double knot in the tails in the back

Knotty Neck Tie

This design begins with a 22" x 22" square silk scarf. Fold the scarf into a triangle by placing the opposite corners together. Roll the triangle into a long narrow strip. Tie a single knot in the center of the strip. Wrap the scarf around the neck with the knot in the front. Tie a double knot in the back of the neck. A great look when you need a pop of color!

See video #55 on my website
www.SilksbyTonya.com

22" x 22" hand painted silk scarf

Step by Step

1) Begin with a small square scarf, fold into a triangle

2) Starting at the point of the triangle, roll the scarf into a narrow strip

3) Tie a single knot in the center of the narrow strip, place the knot on the front of the neck

4) Tie a double knot in the back and tuck the ends in the sides

Do-Rag Head Wrap

This design begins with a 22" x 22" square silk scarf. Fold the scarf into a triangle by joining the opposite corners together. Take the long side of the triangle around the forehead and the point to the back. Tie the tails in the back over the point of the triangle.

Grab your shades and sport this look!

See video #62 on my website
www.SilksbyTonya.com

22"x 22" hand painted silk scarf

Step by Step

1) Begin with a small square scarf and fold it into a triangle

2) Place center of long part of triangle on forehead allowing the point to go to the back

3) Bring the tails to the back

4) Tie tails in a double knot in the back

Chapter 5 - 22" x 90" Scarves

Page 108

Page 109

Page 110

Page 111

Page 112

Page 113

Page 114

Page 115

Page 116

Page 117

Page 118

Page 119

Page 120

Page 121

Page 122

Waist Wrap Top

This design begins with a 22" x 90" silk scarf. Place the center of the scarf around the breast and cross it in the back. Bring the tails to the front and tie them in a double knot.

You look so elegant!

See video #63 on my website
www.SilksbyTonya.com

22" x 90" hand painted silk scarf

Step by Step

1) Begin with a very long scarf

2) Place the center of the scarf over the breast line and take the tails to the back

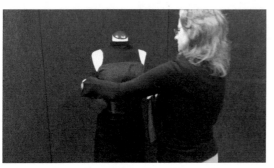

3) Cross the tails in the back and bring them around the body to the front

4) Tie the tails in a double knot just under the breast line

Elegant Neck Wrap

This design begins with a 22" x 90" silk scarf. Drape the scarf around the neck and place one of the tails over the shoulder. Allowing one tail to hang to the back and one to the front.

So elegant….

See video #66 on my website
www.SilksbyTonya.com

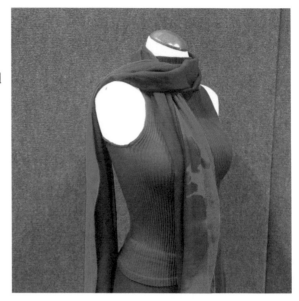

22"x 90" hand painted silk scarf

Step by Step

1) Begin with a long narrow scarf

2) Drape the center of the scarf around the neck allowing the tails to hang down the front

3) Drape the left tail over the right shoulder

Center Tie Wrap

This design begins with a 22" x 90" long silk scarf. Place the center of the scarf around the shoulders and bring the two ends to the front. Tie the tails in the front at the center allowing the tails to hang to the front.

Enjoy your new bathing suit cover up, you look great!

See video #67 on my website
www.SilksbyTonya.com

22" x 90" hand painted silk scarf

Step by Step

1) Begin with a large long scarf

2) Drape the scarf around the back of the shoulders

3) Bring the tails together at the breast line

4) Tie in a double knot to secure at breast line

Shoulder Wrap

This design begins with a 22" x 90" silk scarf. Drape the scarf around the shoulders at the center of the scarf. Allow both tails to hang in the front.

This is an elegant wrap over a simple dress.

See video #70 on my website
www.SilksbyTonya.com

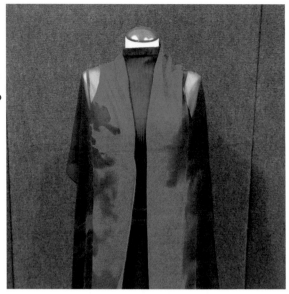

22"x 90" hand painted silk scarf

Step by Step

1) Begin with a long wide scarf

2) Drape the scarf around the body at the center of the scarf

3) Covering the shoulders with the scarf allow the tails to hang in the front

Bathing Suit Cover w/Scarf Pin

This design begins with a 22" x 90" silk scarf. Wrap the scarf around the waste at the center of the scarf. Cross the tails in the front. Take one of the tails around the back of the neck and join the two tails at the top of one shoulder. Attach your scarf pin at the shoulder where the two tails meet.

This bathing suit cover up will turn heads.

See video #71 on my website
www.SilksbyTonya.com

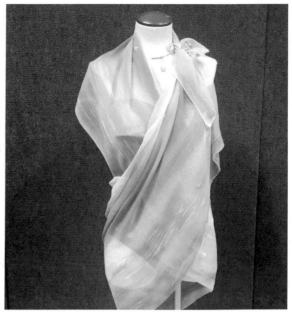

22" x 90" hand painted silk scarf

and hand hammered scarf pin

Step by Step

1) Begin with a very long wide scarf

2) Drape the scarf around the right hip, leaving the front only long enough to reach the left shoulder

3) Wrap the back tail around the front and up over the right shoulder

4) Bring both tails together at the left shoulder and tie in a knot or secure with a scarf pin

Fun Wrap

This design begins with a 22" x 90" silk scarf. Gather the fabric in a bunch and drape the scarf around the neck with one end longer than the other. Wrap the longer of the two ends around the neck once. Place your hand at the loop around the neck, go under the tail that you wrapped around the neck making a loop. Take the opposite tail down through the loop. Tie a double knot at the end of the two tails and place knot behind the neck. Pull the tails down over the shoulders.

See video #72 on my website
www.SilksbyTonya.com

22"x 90" hand painted silk scarf

Step by Step

1) Begin with a very long wide scarf

2) Fold scarf in half with one side longer

3) Wrap the long tail around the neck grabbing one side creating a loop. 4) Draw other tail down through the loop

5) Tie double knot in ends of tails and pull over the head and shoulders

Elegant Dress Wrap

This design begins with a 22" x 90" silk scarf. Wrap the scarf around the neck at the center of the scarf. Wrap one tail over the opposite shoulder allowing it to hang to the back.

Way to take your simple black dress from ok to WOW. Great job!

See video #73 on my website
www.SilksbyTonya.com

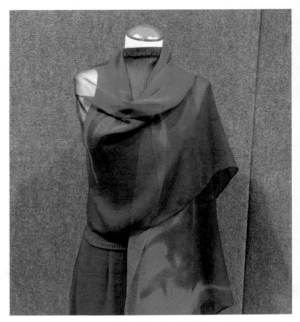

22" x 90" hand painted silk scarf

Step by Step

1) Begin with a long wide scarf

2) Drape scarf over right shoulder

3) Bring back tail around left shoulder and drape it in front

4) Bring the right tail over the left shoulder and allow it to hang down the back

Elegant Dress Shoulder Tie

This design begins with a 22" x 90" silk scarf. Wrap the scarf around your shoulders at the center of the scarf. Take the point of one tail and wrap it around the neck once and allow it to hang forward on the shoulder. Bring the other tail up to meet it and tie a double knot allowing the short tails to hang to the front.

Beautiful job!

See video #74 on my website
www.SilksbyTonya.com

22"x 90" hand painted silk scarf

Step by Step

1) Begin with a long wide scarf

2) Wrap the scarf around the shoulders

3) Take the left tail up over the right shoulder and around the neck

4) Join the right tail to the left at the left shoulder and tie to secure

Bathing Suit Drape

This design begins with a 22" x 90" silk scarf. Wrap the scarf at the center around the shoulders and allow the tails to hang in the front to cover your bathing suit.

Cruise ready! Set sail in style!

See video #76 on my website
www.SilksbyTonya.com

22"x 90" hand painted silk scarf

Step by Step

1) Begin with a long wide scarf

2) Drape the scarf around the shoulders at the center of the scarf

3) Covering the shoulders with the scarf allow the tails to hang in the front

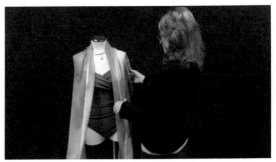

A magnetic clasp could be used just under the breast line to secure

Twisted Shoulder Wrap

This design begins with a 22" x 90" long silk scarf. Fold the scarf in half lengthwise. Take the opposite corners in your hand and drape the scarf on the front. Bring the two opposite ends to the back and tie a double knot.

Beautiful shoulder wrap, great job!

See video #77 on my website
www.SilksbyTonya.com

22" x 90" hand painted silk scarf

Step by Step

1) Begin with a long wide scarf

2) Fold in half length wise

3) Grabbing the opposite corners (top of one side and bottom of the other)

4) Tie a double knot at the back of the neck allowing the twist to hang in the front and over the shoulders

Summer Elegance

This design begins with a 22" x 90" silk scarf. Gather the fabric and place in the front of the neck allowing both tails to hang in the back. Cross the tails in the back and bring them to the front around the breast line. Cross the tails at the breast line and attach your scarf pin to secure.

You are rocking this look….

See video #78 on my website
www.SilksbyTonya.com

22"x 90" hand painted silk scarf

and hand hammered scarf pin

Step by Step

1) Begin with a long wide scarf, gather it into a narrow strip

2) Place the center of scarf around the front of the neck, crossing the tails in the back

3) Bring both tails to the front gathering them together at the breast line

4) Secure with a knot or a scarf pin at breast line

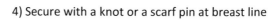

Butterfly Wrap

This design begins with a 22" x 90" long silk scarf. Wrap the scarf around the shoulders at the center of the scarf draping the ends in the front. Take one tail and cross it over the opposite shoulder allowing a length to drape at the neck line. Take the opposite tail and drop it down in the length of drape you left in the front. Adjust the tail hanging in the back and the one hanging in the front to a pleasing fit. Rock this look!

See video #79 on my website
www.SilksbyTonya.com

22" x 90" hand painted silk scarf

Step by Step

1) Begin with a long wide scarf

2) Wrap the scarf around the back of the shoulders allowing both tails to hang in front

3) Bring the left tail over the right shoulder allowing the neck to drape down

4) Take the right tail down through the drape created earlier on the neck

Elegant Cover

This design begins with a 22" x 90" silk scarf. At the center of the scarf wrap it around the waste from the back to the front. Cross the tails over the breasts and drape each one over the opposite shoulder. Allow the tails to hang in the back. The tails can be tied in the back if it seems more comfortable and secure.

Beautiful top, Great job!

See video #80 on my website
www.SilksbyTonya.com

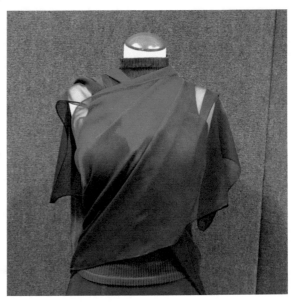

22"x 90" hand painted silk scarf

Step by Step

1) Begin with a long wide scarf

2) Place the scarf around the back

3) Wrapping the left tail around the breast line and up around the right shoulder

4) Wrapping the right tail around the breast line and up around the left shoulder

Shoulder Sash

This design begins with a 22" x 90" long silk scarf. Wrap the scarf around one shoulder and draw both tails to the opposite side. Tie a double knot in the side just under the breast line.

Sophisticated!

See video #86 on my website
www.SilksbyTonya.com

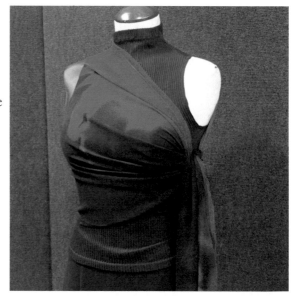

22"x 90" hand painted silk scarf

Step by Step

1) Begin with a long wide scarf

2) Drape the center of the scarf over the right shoulder

3) Bring both tails together at the left side just below the breast line

4) Tie a loose double knot in both tails at the left side

Cruise Ready Wrap w/ Scarf Pin

This design begins with a 22" x 90" long silk scarf. Wrap the scarf around the body under the arm and bring both ends to the opposite shoulder. Draw up a length at the shoulder and secure the scarf pin at the front of the shoulder.

Beautiful Job! You Rock!

See video #92 on my website
www.SilksbyTonya.com

22"x 90" hand painted silk scarf

and hand hammered scarf pin

Step by Step

1) Begin with a long wide scarf

2) Wrap the scarf around the left side and gather both ends together at the right shoulder

3) Pull up about 6 inches or so at the right shoulder

4) Secure tabs just created at the right shoulder with a scarf pin

About The Author

Tonya Butcher grew up in a small town in West Virginia and moved to Virginia where she met the love of her life. Tonya was blessed with 5 wonderful children and 11 amazing grandchildren.

Tonya has a true gift and artistic passion. In 2008 she was blessed with a beautiful grand-daughter that sparked something inside her to begin her artistic journey, and an exciting journey it has been. Not long after this, Tonya said goodbye to her accounting career to become a full time artist. Her love of vibrant clean color comes out in her beautiful designs. She gets lost in the creation process and enjoys helping others learn to create a new favorite look.

Tonya enjoys teaching art at her art studio in Northern Virginia.

Tonya's art can be viewed online at www.TonyaButcher.com and her silk designs may be viewed at www.SilksbyTonya.com

"We are all created in the image of the father and I embrace his presence in my life. I encourage you to spend some time today in his powerful presence". Tonya Butcher

Made in the USA
Columbia, SC
16 March 2024

33158487R00069